DARPA
FLAMES OF FEAR

Darpa Flames of Fear by Manuel Pelaez

ISBN 978-1-955136-39-6 (Paperback)
ISBN 978-1-955136-40-2 (Hardback)

This book is written to provide information and motivation to readers. Its purpose is not to render any type of psychological, legal, or professional advice of any kind. The content is the sole opinion and expression of the author, and not necessarily that of the publisher.

Printed in the United States of America.

New Leaf Media, LLC
175 S. 3rd Street, Suite 200
Columbus, OH 43215
www.thenewleafmedia.com

MANUEL PELAEZ

CHAPTER 1

Time stands still whenever anyone mentions the name Siria, try not to say it too loud. Absolutely no one wants to be in her presence, it will definitely become a fatal encounter. The fires of hell burn in her eyes, the fury, the rage, the unbelievable quest for revenge, all these things grew inside her. Siria, knows that anger alone will not be enough, there is a reason why her late father the messiah and one of the most intelligent scientific minds, a former robotic engineering scientist of DARPA, choose her as his predecessor. Siria, herself has acquired all the knowledge from her legendary father, highly trained in science in every sector. She is also surrounded by loyalists that without any hesitation will give their lives willingly to protect her. Siria, stands on top of the throne heir to the messiah her father, the late Ron Ben Ruckman.

Chapter 2

The following are the developments of the storyline, first challenge is to find out exactly who is responsible for the attack that killed both of her parents and the scientists working with her father. The next challenge will be how to execute a master plan to revenge their deaths. Next challenge will be to put together a team worthy of this tasks, Siria, also knows that she must show she is worthy of her leadership. She must prove that she has a strong hand and intelligence for everyone to follow her into futures to come. Siria's strategies moving forward shall be the exact opposite of her late father with doses of heavy revenge embedded deep inside her heart. There shall not be any more speeches in front of thousands of followers, as was common with her late father (the messiah).

Chapter 3

DARPA, shall feel our wrath and our pain, we shall bring hell to them indirectly, with precision attacks. The strategy moving forward shall be moving to different locations randomly. DARPA, will not be able to target our locations, after a considerable amount of time the scientists that surround Siria have determined that the chemical bomb involved in her parent's deaths, was in fact DARPA. The scientists loyal to Siria, carefully broke down the chemical dispositions and technologies. The elements involved in the chemical bomb and the way it was deployed, can only point to one intelligence, that being DARPA. It is concluded at this time that DARPA ordered an attack on the temple, as revenge for the attack that occurred on their compounds. Such news only enrages Siria even more, lord have mercy on DARPA. The awesome power of DARPA worldwide, it would be an understatement describing the most advanced technologies ever witnessed by anyone.

CHAPTER 4

Autonomous technologies that seem as extreme fiction, but this highly classified top-secret powerhouse entity is beyond realistic. The autonomous super soldiers are a force to be reckoned with, capabilities equipped with high energy kilowatt lasers. The autonomous spider super soldiers are also equipped with high energy kilowatt lasers. Precision targeting, infrared technologies, reinforced armor, extremely maneuverable. On land or sea, DARPA is the symbol of excellence, the autonomous underwater weaponized drones. The lethal autonomous supersonic drones, are the premier advancement. Capabilities, equipped with hypersonic missile systems, precision high energy kilowatt laser systems. Infrared night technologies, Mach supersonic speeds, advanced maneuverability's, land and liftoff advancements. Advanced tracking systems, defensive stealth capabilities, heat signature detections. DARPA compounds are highly classified and an impenetrable fortress, each compound is in unknown locations, highly classified. DARPA is the breakthrough of advanced technologies in every scientific sector, medical, warfare, space explorations, ocean aquatic technologies. The smartest, most advanced scientist the world has ever seen.

CHAPTER 5

Meanwhile, Siria's strategic coordinated attack plans are being reviewed by her top loyalists. The strategic coordinated attacks are as follows , complete acknowledgment of DARPA's (UNI-WORLD) structures worldwide. ARCTIC-SPHERE, TROPIC-JUNGLES, THE-PLAINS, RIVER-BASINS, WILDERNESS. These are the different habitats within DARPA's (UNI-WORLD), the different countries involved are the following. Canada, Siberia, parts of Alaska, parts of Africa, Madagascar, Australia, Costa Rica. The DARPA compounds are completely off the grid and in unknown locations. The information gathered so for that these compounds are somewhere in the dessert of Nevada, dessert of Texas, somewhere in Russia, and China. Besides the United States of America, Russia and China have their own version of DARPA as well, these facilities are highly classified, so little information is known. Due to the severity of climate change many habitable lands have disappeared. As a result, improved sophisticated tunnel systems were designed, the marvel of civil engineering. Extending through many regions underground tunnels that extend for miles, flood prevention, upgraded sewers, electrical systems, state of the art technologies were built. The strategic coordinated attack plans will be done in waves, a specific timeline, overwhelming force, entry and exit coordination's.

CHAPTER 6

The sect group of believers will infiltrate the local government public works department to gather intel on the underground tunnel system maps. Each manhole will also be marked with special fluorescent paint which glows in the dark also. This will take place in nearby malls where many civilians are gathered, the first wave will hide IED (improvised explosive devices). Inside the public restrooms a IED (improvised explosive devices) will explode at the same timeline as the others, even though, they will be placed in different time zones. This event will be heard extremely loud throughout the malls, causing chaos. At this point the civilians shopping and walking around the malls will run towards the exits. The second wave will be strategically waiting outside some specific exits, at this time armed sect believers with automatic weapons will fire barrages of bullets into the crowds escaping. Targeting an untold number of civilians outside, every minute counts, because SUV (ep) electric powered will be parked close to the sect believers to enter and escape. The main purpose for this event to take place is to draw out the autonomous super soldiers that will assist the authorities. The escape plan, will be as follows, the SUV (ep) electric powered will drive from the malls to where the manholes are located. The reason for this exit plan, prior training exercises underground the manhole routes. The underground paths are a maze of tunnels leading to a safer exit plan, the group of sect believers will be wearing special suits. The main purpose for such precautionary measures is to become hidden from the autonomous supersonic drones. The special suits the group of sect believers will be wearing blocks body heat signatures, the underground tunnels will make the sect believers invisible to the autonomous supersonic drones. At each exit from the manholes there will be vehicles waiting for them, once they exit the underground tunnels. The group of sect believers will unzip their special suits, hiding them inside the SUV (ep) electric powered vehicles and drive away to appear as normal. The group of sect believers will also hide their automatic weapons in the SUV (ep) electric powered vehicles.

The third wave, known as the death squad, these individuals are completely suicidal. Their main purpose is to target the autonomous super solders, this is easier said than done. The death squad will be equipped with FIM-92 stingers, firing from the shoulders. Their main adjective is to aim at the autonomous super soldier's limbs, exploding the autonomous super soldier's limbs will incapacitate their mobilities. A coordinated stealth attack is crucial, because the autonomous super soldiers have advanced weaponry also. The timeline is extremely important, the death squad will be wearing special suits also. The minute the authorities arrive with the assistance of the autonomous super soldiers.

Chapter 7

The death squad will exit their vehicles already parked in designated areas in the parking lots of the malls. To make things crystal clear, many authorities will be injured also in the blasts. The death squad primary objectives are to target the autonomous super soldiers. The purpose of causing these major events at the malls, is basically because the malls are specifically located close to (UNI-WORLD). Each (UNI-WORLD) serves as a base for DARPA's assets to be stationed, there are always a heavy presence of autonomous super soldiers, autonomous supersonic drones, besides cadets and other autonomous cargo vehicles there. With no doubt, the autonomous super soldiers will be assisting the authorities. The lethal autonomous supersonic drones arrive afterwards, leaving a small window of opportunities. Once, the autonomous supersonic drones arrive its game over, the death squad don't have an escape plan but they also have trained prior to exactly the manholes are located. If by some miracle, any of the death squad are able to escape, they have previously trained in the exits of the underground tunnels. They also know that a vehicle will be parked close to the exits, the keys of the vehicles are placed inside hidden. The rendezvous points, now, we will carefully examine the exit plan after the events. Two different regions will be targeted, this includes Canada, and Siberia. In these regions (UNI-WORLD) has extensive habitats, even though, (UNI-WORLD) itself will not be targeted. The nearby malls are the main focus, the main goal is to have one small cargo plane at each location waiting in an air field, but the location in Siberia is questionable because there's hardly any intel on this highly classified location.

CHAPTER 8

Let us now give a full description of the group of sect believers which are now led by Siria (daughter of the late messiah Ron Ben Ruckman). It is also important to understand their cause and how they are financed. The believers are 100% loyal to ancient scripture, denouncing the modern world ideologies. They were organized by radicalized extremists and have grown worldwide. Their cause is well financially encrypted into a secret society. Their temples are mostly located in the Middle East, but they have believers in many regions. Modern medicine is accepted in their beliefs, but they view DARPA and the modern world as a poison to civilizations. Intel and intelligence data show that a major event will be taking place which the attacks timeline will be orchestrated and executed.

Chapter 9

The anniversary of the solar power stations in space, this event will be a monumental moment in human history, Important note, with endless supply of energy our world can have EV chargers, electric vehicle supply equipment (EVSE) stations worldwide even in remote areas. This challenge was only made possible with the coordination of the superpower nations. The United States, China and Russia, leading the way to space. Of course, many other nations are also involved, the prime adjective when designing these solar power stations in space was to provide the energy needs for planet Earth. Let's explain in details how this is possible, solar power stations in space, photovoltaic array converts the sunlight into electricity. Electromagnetic radiation non-ionizing radiation frequencies, solar power stations in space could supply the world with limitless energy. Giant space-based solar farms, photovoltaic array is composed of lightweight, deployable structure made of many smaller "solar satellites" that could easily connect together in space to form much larger array and "harvest sunlight". Orbiting 22,000 miles above the Earth and "beam" the energy back down to the surface. Generating a constant flow of 2,000 gigawatts of power, harvesting renewable energy from the sun and outer space at the same time. Severe climate change has forced the nations of our world to work together to solve major crisis worldwide. The major nations military space forces and classified companies involved in these achievements are as follows. The United States Space Force (Guardians), National Aeronautics and Space Administration (NASA), Defense Advanced Research Project Agency (DARPA), The People's Liberation Army Strategic Support Force (PLASSF), The Russian Space Forces. Many more nations are involved directly or indirectly with solutions to crisis worldwide. DARPA's visions of bringing together many nations participating to make our world's future much better has become a reality.

CHAPTER 10

The anniversary of the solar power stations in space will be celebrated world-wide, it will be seen on television and radio. Jumbotron oversized television screens which were already placed at major shopping malls and stadiums will also sponsor this monumental event. The actual ceremonies will be held in three different locations which are highly classified militarized Space Launch Complexes. Locations are the following, Alaska Pacific Spaceport Complex, and Kazakhstan Baikonur Cosmodrome, and China National Space Administration (CNSA) Wenchang Space Launch Site, these locations are somewhere in unknown destinations, according to updated data. These locations used to be known but with severe ocean water level rise due to climate change entire regions have vanished. At the ceremonies the military of these launch sites will be present, DARPA personal will be present also. DARPA will assist the military to secure the perimeters around the launch sites. Each superpower nations have their own version of DARPA, autonomous lethal supersonic drones will be mostly activated. The attacks by the group of sect believers are planned and orchestrated with this in mind. The sect believer's intel and data show that the autonomous super soldiers will be activated to assist the local authorities. This will create a temporary timeline window of opportunity to strike full force until the autonomous lethal supersonic drones arrive. The group of sect believers need to move quickly and escape to be underground in the tunnels before this happens.

CHAPTER 11

Let's backtrack now to explain how exactly the death squad was formed in every detail. The main temple is located in a unknown secret location somewhere in the Middle East. One early morning, a small group of grunts which are known as street beggars did not at the time know about what was the temple's purpose. It was raining heavily and no guards were seen anywhere, this small group of eight individuals. At the time these grunts range from ages 16 to 20 years old, they live in the neighboring town. This group of grunts are known to be begging for money and sometimes steal things like food or anything they can get. Without any knowledge of the temple the small group of grunts attempt to climb over the walls. One by one they climb over, thinking in their minds that they are about to find food, and other resources. The heavy rain continued; they ran across the courtyard trying not to make loud noises. When suddenly, they were surrounded by armed believers holding machine guns. The group of sect believers are like quiet ghosts, they don't speak much. Now, the small group of grunts will face their destinies, they are lost souls from the streets with plenty of hardships in their lives. The small group of grunts are on their knees on the floor waiting for Siria to make her presence known. Before Siria makes her appearance, let's backtrack to an incident that took place when she was a teenager starting her role as the supreme leader. After her late father's death who everyone followed as the messiah, Siria became the supreme leader. She was a young leader and needed to prove herself worthy of this role. One day a servant confronted her which is disrespectful, and exchanged words with her. Siria, told her loyalists to take her outside and kneel her on the ground. The next scene is extremely graphic, Siria, grabbed a razor-sharp sword and with one strong swing she severed the servant's head completely off, the loyalists standing around noticed how the body was trembling on the ground afterwards. Siria, had her loyalists boil the servant's head to be reduced to a mini skull. Knowledge of shrinking techniques were culturally shared by generations. Siria, always has that small skull with her to remind her that leadership comes with a strong hand. The moment Siria makes her presence known to address the situation at the moment taking a seat. Siria speaks, "only one of you speak in behalf of everyone else". One hand rises up and speaks, "my name is Isiah, we kneel in front of you completely at your mercy. My entire existence is a miracle as everyone is this group also, our families suffered from the new world ideologies. They were slowly killed off one by one, the sorrow runs deep in our veins. All we have left is to truly embrace the old-world prophecies, I do not lie and we are ready to parish by your hands". Siria replies, " your group is either the bravest souls I know, or the stupidest. I will have your stories checked out and if there's anything questionable. Expect your skulls to be with me forever, as a reminder to testing my judgment". After some time passed, the small group of grunts were detained and awaiting their fate.

CHAPTER 12

One day, the loyalists tell them that their stories checked out, and to follow them. The small group of grunts kneel inside the courtyard in the presence of Siria. Siria speaks, "each of your stories checked out, you were all left in the streets to survive and beg for whatever people can give you. Your families suffered in the hands of the modern world ideologies, let it be known as of this day you will become part of an elite group called the death squad. This group tasks are completely suicidal, we will train you, we will teach you the old ancient prophecies. In short, each of you shall become part of our family, you Isiah, the one who speaks for your group shall be their leader". The small group of grunts led by Isiah waste no time to start training, they shall gain knowledge of weapons, explosives, overall, 100% loyalty and discipline. They shall become perfect military soldiers for the cause, becoming believers themselves. After many years of vigorous training, mentally, physically, and spiritually, the death squad is now formed. Preparation in forming a squad that will be feared and completely fearless was a crucial role in the planned attacks. While the death squad was being formed, infiltrators located in the two regions where attacks are going to be executed are put in place.

CHAPTER 13

Let's explain how the group of sect believers can penetrate these regions and gather intelligence and crucial intel for a successful outcome. Let's begin with Siberia, which was originally thought to be impossible, the sect believers were lucky in obtaining two others that believe in their cause. Years before the actual attack happens, a small group of sect believers infiltrate the region, traveling by commercial plane with the proper documentations. They are met by a couple of others inside Siberia, one of them can easily acquire the underground tunnel maps and road maps. One even works in the company that built the underground tunnel systems. I want to emphasize that these facilities are not militarized related structures. The Russian military are not involved in the civil engineering systems, the Russian version of DARPA compounds are located inside Russia. Those facilities are highly classified and in unknown locations, I also want to emphasize that not everyone worldwide agrees with advanced technologies running our planet. This is exactly why the believers are able to obtain vital intel and information in different regions. Once the small group of sect believers are put in place, they act perfectly normal blending in and waiting for further instructions. I want to emphasize, that the two other sect believers that have been living in Siberia will leave the country prior to the attacks, this will assure that nothing will be compromised once an official investigation begins. The explosive devices that will be used in the attacks are modern, mostly undetectable, meaning the materials can easily go through any metal detectors. The group of sect believers are well trained with knowledge and helped by two others in the region which also believe in ancient prophecies. In Siberia there are shopping centers or malls miles away from (UNI-WORLD), the manholes which lead to the underground tunnels are close by also. Everything is in place waiting for the anniversary event in the upcoming months. The sect believers acquire jobs inside the shopping center or malls, and around the area, they also live in the area, getting help from the others already established there.

CHAPTER 14

At the same time this is happening in Siberia, a small group of sect believers are put in place in Canada, also, traveling by commercial plane with proper documentations, there they are joined by a couple of others who believe in their cause as well. The sect believers are able to obtain the underground tunnel map systems and road maps, there is a (UNI-WORLD) nearby with its amazing habitats. Shopping centers or malls are close by also, it's basically, the same blueprint in each region. The sect believers acquire jobs inside the shopping center or mall and around the area, getting places to live with assistance from the others already established there. I want to emphasize, that the two other sect believers will be leaving the country prior to the attacks by commercial airlines, nothing will be put in jeopardy once an official investigation begins. There are no DARPA compounds inside Canada, instead, these highly classified facilities are located in the United States. It is important to know that there are abandoned airfields located nearby. In each region, the anniversary event which will take place at highly classified militarized Space Launch Complexes. These facilities are not nearby (UNI-WORLD), or the shopping centers or malls, the window of opportunity and timeline is apparent to a successful outcome. Please note, the death squad are divided into four out of eight individuals to be among the other sect believers, this small group of individuals are infiltrated into the communities but they stay among themselves, due to the meditative state of mind preparing for the ultimate sacrifices. Another group of eight sect believers will also be divided in four individuals which will be assembled as one driver, one explosive expert, two actual shooters carrying automatic weapons, the total amount of sect believers and death squad members in total are sixteen individuals. The following is a full description on how the following events unfold, in different time zones and different regions, all occurring on the same day, please, be aware that some scenes are very graphic in nature. After years of preparation and planning of the strategic upcoming attacks, the worldwide event has finally arrived.

CHAPTER 15

Somewhere in the middle of fall, in Alaska inside the highly classified Pacific Spaceport Complex at approximately 06:00 hours the celebrations begin bright and early due to extended daylight hours, it will last until 23:00 hours. DARPA and CIA Director Jones is orbiting inside the newly designed United States Space Station. This honor is granted to him along with other military colleagues, a front row seat of witnessing the giant space-solar farms or solar power stations in outer space first hand. What an exciting moment to actually see such an enormous structure up close. Everything is being televised throughout the day and night, a pre-record speech is also being broadcast. Security measures are as follows, the United States Space Force (Guardians), will be the watchdogs in space, Defense Advanced Research Project Agency (DARPA), will secure things on the ground. Providing its elite autonomous lethal supersonic drone forces, the United States military will also be present. The following prerecorded speech is Director Jones giving a very emotional and inspirational message worldwide in different languages.

CHAPTER 16

Director Jones speaks, "today, I stand here with my colleagues in their respected fields. Celebrating worldwide our greatest achievements on our planet, together we have collectively solved our world's problems and bring brighter futures for everyone to bear witness what advanced technologies can accomplish. Today, we as a planet celebrate together, today, we are proud and can only dream of what's ahead. Let us celebrate our technological advancements and what was once impossible, we as a modern world family have made it possible". After this extremely powerful speech an eruption of applauses are heard everywhere. This prerecorded speech broadcasts every hour, it is also joined by other speeches afterwards from the Kazakhstan Baikonur Cosmodrome and the China National Space Administration (CNSA) Wenchang Space Launch Site. At the same time the speech is being televised, the two other sect believers are at the airport boarding their flight to the Middle East a friendly country, afterwards, they will be transported to an unknown location in the Middle East to join their brothers and sisters in the cause.

Chapter 17

In Canada, moments before 09:00 hours the believers commence their operation. One of the sect believers is carrying shopping store bags right into the shopping center or mall. Walking right into the restroom, there a shopping bag is left inside the stall. The door to the stall a small flat bar is glued slightly above where the lock is located, the glue dries fast and it will appear as if the stall door is completely locked. The shopping center or mall has many civilians inside looking around at the Jumbotron and other screens televising the event. The sect believer walks out normally with a shopping bag to appear less suspicious and exits, at approximately 09:00 hours the bomb explodes inside the restroom. Anyone inside the restroom at that time is killed instantly, a very loud noise echoes throughout the shopping center or mall. Instantly, the sect believer enters the SUV (ep) electric powered vehicle parked right in front of the exit of the shopping center or mall. Without wasting any time starts to put on the special suit which is a whole piece that can be easily worn on top of regular clothes. Only the shoes must be taken off, at this same time, two of the sect believers open their doors carrying automatic weapons. When suddenly large crowds of citizens are exiting the shopping center or mall because of the explosion. The sect believers start to fire live rounds at the large crowds, many are killed and wounded instantly. The sect believers with automatic weapons quickly enter the SUV (ep) electric powered vehicle and the driver spins off with no hesitation. The SUV (ep) electric powered vehicle moves quickly through the back roads to avoid traffic straight to the location of the manhole, sticking strictly to the plan. At this time, all hell is breaking loose, the authorities receive news of this emergency crisis. The authorities are assisted by the autonomous super soldiers that are dispatched from (UNI-WORLD) nearby. At this time, another SUV (ep) electric powered vehicle quietly positions itself close to where all the trauma is taking place. Inside the SUV (ep) electric powered vehicle are the four individuals which are known as the death squad. First, the authorities arrive police together with the fire department crews, fire rescue vehicles (ep) electric powered. Shortly, after that the autonomous super soldiers arrive, their presence is something to witness. The autonomous super soldiers were already on route to be placed at the shopping center or mall for security measures. DARPA, mobilizes autonomous cargo vehicles to transport these advanced technological soldiers. Please note, that worldwide all gas operated vehicles were discontinued to salvage our world from further climate change damage.

Chapter 18

At this moment, the four individuals known as the death squad exit the SUV (ep) electric powered vehicle each carrying modern FIM-92 stingers. They place the FIM-92 stingers on their shoulders, before firing at the autonomous super soldiers. Isiah, the leader of the death squad is among the four individuals, he yells out, "today we go straight to hell, we bring the autonomous super soldiers with us". Within seconds, the four individuals of the death squad and the autonomous super soldiers exchange fire. The explosions hit the autonomous super soldiers on the limbs destroying quite a few of them. At the same time, some of the authorities are severely injured also, the autonomous super soldiers were able to fire back. The explosions exploded the SUV (ep) electric powered vehicle and killed three of the death squad members. The explosion itself causes shrapnel to fly everywhere, hitting Isiah in many places of his body. At this point, the rest of the authorities including police and fire hide behind vehicles. The autonomous super soldiers are disabled with missing limbs and damaged. Isiah, limping and wounded he manages to take a tri-wheel scooter (ep) electric powered which the parking lot is full of, these vehicles are the preferred transportation for most individuals traveling alone. These tri-wheel scooters (ep) electric powered can be turned on by touch bottom and Isiah has acquired knowledge from his past on how to take these scooters. Isiah, always keeps a handgun with him always, with the scooter (ep) electric powered he can easily zigzag through traffic. Isiah, quickly escapes driving the scooter (ep) electric powered, towards the manhole to make a quick exit. Moments before, the sect believers exit their SUV (ep) electric powered vehicle and open the manhole using a metal tool. They quickly climb down the ladder into the darkness of the underground tunnels. Leaving the manhole cover opened and using flashlights walking fast through the tunnels.

CHAPTER 19

At this time, word gets to the Alaska Pacific Spaceport Complex, where quickly the autonomous lethal supersonic drones are already on route towards the emergency crisis. More autonomous super soldiers are also dispatched from (UNI-WORLD), the word reaches Director Jones at the newly designed United States Space Station. Director Jones speaks in anger, " what in the hell is happening, this group takes crazy to a completely whole other level. I want the full force of DARPA, and other agencies to rain down hell itself to these bastards. I want updates on everything in real time as they develop, we will not tolerate such rebellious acts and will impose the domestic terrorism act". Immediately after his angry words, Director Jones cut short his participation in the event and will be transported to the Earth's surface. Once he returns to the Earth's surface, he will attend briefings on current developmental situations.

CHAPTER 20

Moments before, Isiah, manages to get to the manhole that is already uncovered. Even in pain and limping he knows he must climb down the ladder and somehow make contact with the four sect believers which have a head start. He grabs the small device he received for emergency purposes to make contact if need be. He presses the button and yells out trying to continue forward, he is equipped with a small power light. One of the sect believers hears the echoes from his voice, and hears the beacon flashing from the emergency device. The one sect believer turns back quickly to help out, this emergency procedure was practiced in their plan. Please note, absolutely none of the sect believers including the death squad members have cellphones with them. These are emergency measures knowing DARPA can track these devices, at no point any communication devices will be on them when boarding the small cargo plane. Time is extremely crucial to escape because the autonomous supersonic drones are traveling at high speeds from the Pacific Spaceport Complex to Canada. Since most of DARPA's elite autonomous lethal supersonic drone forces were providing security on the ground in the event. Their other elite autonomous lethal supersonic drone forces are also in the DARPA compounds which are much further away. Quickly, the one sect believer makes contact with Isiah and helps him move faster throughout the tunnel system. The three other sect believers have already exited the underground tunnels and get into the vehicle (ep) electric powered. They are very much aware of the situation unfolding with the other sect believer and an impatiently waiting every minute. Finally, the other one sect believer almost carrying Isiah out of the underground tunnel gets more help from the other three sect believers to bring in Isiah inside the vehicle (ep) electric powered and drive away. They try their best to comfort Isiah with patching up the bleeding but he is obviously in pain, they all have the special suits on to block them from any heat signatures. Quickly driving off towards the rendezvous point where the abandoned airfield is located. It's a short trip and they all quickly leave the vehicle (ep) electric powered there and enter the small cargo plane to takeoff. The pilot doesn't waste any time and takes off from the runway to take flight towards their destination somewhere in the Middle East. Shortly after takeoff and distancing themselves from the abandoned airfield.

Chapter 21

Just in the nick of time, the autonomous lethal supersonic drones arrive hovering around everywhere. Their presence changes everything, they are well equipped with all kinds of detectors. Their scans don't pick up on any heat signatures but they do detect a small blood trail. Their scans can detect the small blood trail from the shopping center or mall to the manhole. They can also follow the trail of small blood throughout the underground tunnels. Immediately, after that point at a distance the small blood trail stops, now, their scans can follow the tire marks from the vehicle (ep) electric powered. Their scans indicate that the vehicle (ep) electric powered exited at the abandoned airfield where the tracks stop. Their scans pick up no more small blood trail, but indicates that a plane took off leaving tracks on the runway. By the time all the scanning was being processed it took some time in developing. The small cargo plane has made a significant amount of flight time and was able to reach its destination. Full reports will be given to Director Jones in real time at the briefing and a full investigation has already begun. I want to emphasize, that before these events take place the two believers inside Siberia that have been living there for years and were established will be leaving the country by commercial airlines to a friendly Middle East country where afterwards they will be transported to an unknown destination to join their brothers and sisters in the same cause. Not taking any chances or leaving any traces when an official investigation occurs.

CHAPTER 22

Important note, all the following events are occurring on the same day and time, but in different time zones, this eliminates any precautionary measures taken by the joint nations involved. The celebrations extend across our world first at the Kazakhstan Baikonur Cosmodrome starting bright and early at 06:00 hours, it will last until 23:00 hours. Led by the Strategic Support Force, the Russian Space Forces a branch of the Russian Aerospace Forces, Russian Foundation for Advanced Research Projects. This highly classified militarized facility has Jumbotron scenes and a heavy presence of military leaders all present for the grand event. This event is all day and night, security on the ground is provided by Russia's own version of DARPA. Their elite autonomous lethal supersonic drone forces are present, after hours pass by, still morning at the Wenchang Space Launch Site. China National Space Administration (CNSA), The Commission for Science, Technology and Industry for National Defense (COSTIND; Chinese. The celebrations for this historical event will be in full force at this highly classified militarized facility. COSTIND) China's version of DARPA, will provide security on the ground with their autonomous supersonic drone forces. The Chinese military will also be present, Jumbotron screens are televising the grand event. In a joint venture between Russia and China from outer space inside the newly designed Tiangong Space Station. The leaders of DARPA in both countries along with other military colleagues, are observing up close the giant space solar stations. Throughout the region prerecorded speeches are being heard everywhere, these historical speeches in their original languages and translated into other languages also.

Chapter 23

The speeches are as follows in Russian, today, "we join other nations comrades. Together we have achieved greatness, our world is now healing from our mistakes. We move forward with technological advancements, joined by the greatest scientific minds. Together we bear witness to history and a world worth saving, let us remember this day". Next in Chinese, "today we celebrate our greatest accomplishments in advanced technologies for one sole purpose to save our only planet from future climate change damage. With this in mind our nations work together for the common good, together we have solved major crisis and will continue in this in this endeavor. This day shall be written in our history and humanity should be proud". The same day, many hours afterwards at night time in Siberia, in a shopping center or mall, it opens at 09:00 hours until 23:00 hours.

CHAPTER 24

The following events take place moments before 21:00 hours, two SUV's (ep) electric powered enter simultaneously the parking lot of the mall. Positioning themselves accordingly, one parks right in front of the mall entrance. The other vehicle is close by, the door opens and one of the sect believers gets out with shopping bags. Starts walking towards the entrance doors which are over ten feet tall and wide, this design structure is for the autonomous super soldiers standing over eight feet tall to enter and exit easily. Each autonomous super soldier have bulky builds with considerable weight but extremely versatile, well-armed and equipped with sophisticated Ground Reaction Force (GRF), Zero Moment Point (ZMP), military grade footpads for balancing and walking. The minute the sect believer walks inside the shopping center or mall, one security guard notices the sect believer moving towards the restrooms. The security guard confronts the sect believer before entering the restrooms, this situation unfolds close to the doors of the shopping center or mall. The security guard asks for the receipts of the items in the bag, an altercation occurs. Some spectators are at a distance watching them exchange words, this leads to a physical altercation. The security guard attempts to grab his gun, the sect believer stabs him with a small razor-sharp knife. Multiple stabs in the neck area drops the security guard onto the ground, at this point the sect believer yells out, "Siria". The sect believer presses the detonator, a giant explosion happens with such a force that the exit and entrance doors are blown into pieces. The glass and shrapnel flying everywhere, the loud noise echoes throughout the shopping center or mall. Everyone that was close to the blast is killed instantly, the large crowds of civilians run in the other direction towards the other exits.

CHAPTER 25

At this time, some of the autonomous super soldiers that were patrolling inside the shopping center or mall, head towards the where the blast occurred. A few autonomous super soldiers patrolling inside the shopping center or mall and outside perimeters. The autonomous super soldiers were already on the premises because of the time, as they move towards the area. The sheer chaos of people leaving the shopping center or mall is everywhere. The moment the super soldiers arrive at the blast area, to observe the damages. Moments before all these events are unfolding, the sect believers outside notice not only the destruction of the blast but instantly losing one of their own. They can clearly see the large crowds going in the opposite direction towards other exits. At this time, they decide to leave while they can, automatic weapons are useless against the autonomous super soldiers, the other SUV (ep) electric powered with the four members of the death squad take their position right in front of where the blast occurred. Let me add, that the damaged area is still burning and there's smoke everywhere.

CHAPTER 26

The moment the vehicle is parked all four doors open and the four members of the death squad get out with each of them carrying modern FIM-92 stingers. The moment the autonomous super soldiers are gathered they are met with the four members of the death squad. They instantly fire the FIM-92 stingers onto the autonomous super soldiers. The autonomous super soldiers are quick to respond, exchanging fire with multiple explosions. The autonomous super soldiers are able to fire back, in one moment, severe damages to the limbs of the autonomous super soldiers are disabled. The autonomous super soldiers manage to instantly disintegrate the four members of the death squad. As this was happening, the sect believers in the other vehicle manage to fire their automatic weapons at the crowds escaping in the other exit. The sect believers are met with security guards firing back at them outside. This exchange of fire hits and kills the driver of the sect believers, at this time the two other sect believers take charge of the situation. The vehicle drives away taking the back roads to avoid traffic, driving straight towards the manhole and the underground tunnels. While all these events are happening in real time, the emergency crisis reaches the authorities and are dispatched to the scene. All police and fire units are on route, and word reaches the Kazakhstan Baikonur Cosmodrome and the Wenchang Space Launch Site. The emergency crisis also reaches the newly designed Tiangong Space Station in outer space. When the word reaches The Commission for Science, Technology and Industry for National Defense (COSTIND) Chinese and Russian Foundation for Advanced Research Projects. These highly classified organizations are China's and Russia's version of DARPA, the leaders of both nations receive the news. They response kindly with anger, (translated in English), "this is unacceptable, I want minute to minute updates and bring them dead or severely wounded to face justice". The full force of DARPA is unleashed, the fleet of autonomous lethal supersonic drones are on route. More autonomous super soldiers are also dispatched from (UNI-WORLD) in Siberia nearby the shopping center or mall.

CHAPTER 27

In one moment, the two other believers reach their location with their vehicle riddled with bullet holes. They leave the vehicle there and can clearly see the manhole marked in fluorescent paint which glows in the dark. Using a metal tool to open the manhole, they quickly go into the underground tunnels with powerful flashlights. They don't waste any time in moving quickly through the tunnels, they cross easily and climb out of the underground tunnels. They exit and the other vehicle (ep) electric powered is there with keys hidden inside. Time is crucial, they quickly drive off towards the abandoned airfield, when they arrive at the abandoned airfield which is a short trip. They quickly board the small cargo plane and the pilot takes off the runway. At this point, the time where any communication from the others passed by, they know the others are gone. The cargo plane takes off quickly, meanwhile, the authorities have arrived at the shopping center or mall to extinguish the fires, and access all the damages. By the time the autonomous lethal supersonic drones arrive from Kazakhstan to Siberia. The small cargo plane makes significant flight time separating their distance. Important note, both pilots which are part of both attacks escape our part of sect believers and their beliefs. Both small cargo planes are wiped clean after landing to rid any evidence and instruments. Once both small cargo planes land at an abandoned airfield somewhere in the Middle East, a small group of sect believers on the ground waiting go into action. Two SUV vehicles (ep) electric powered one will transport Isiah and the six sect believers to get immediate medical attention. The other SUV (ep) electric powered has a few individuals to take out some crucial instruments or any evidence including fingerprints. After everything is complete quickly following a strict timeline, both vehicles shall reunite in a secretive location inside the Middle East.

Chapter 28

In a secretive location somewhere in the Middle East, Siria, addresses the sect believers before going underground in hiding from DARPA and military personnel. Isiah, is getting much needed medical attention, his medical status reaches the temple. The medical staff's report, he is a lucky man, he will undergo surgeries to remove several pieces of metal shrapnel from his body, no major arteries were severed, he shall heal after the surgeries, he will need some rehabilitation, the other six believers are fine also, some minor surgeries, some healing. Siria speaks to the sect believers briefly, after walking out to the courtyard, everything goes silent when Siria makes her appearance known. Siria speaks, "Isiah, is in bondage and recovering from injuries, after immediate surgeries. After sustaining significant injuries, he needs time to heal, the other six believers are also fine after minor surgeries and some time to heal. let us remember this day and honor the brave souls that were lost. Each of their names shall be written on the memorial of the brave, every year this day shall be remembered and celebrated. On this day, we brought an overwhelming show of force and hell to DARPA, let it be known that on this day I name Isiah as my head bodyguard. It is impressive, what the entire group did especially Isiah and the six believers as the only sole survivors from their brothers and sisters. From this day forward, the bravery from the entire group souls, Isiah and the six other believers have demonstrated, shall become the mark of our existence".

Chapter 29

Meanwhile, after a short time passed, in a joint venture between The United States, Russia, and China, top secret agencies DARPA, will conduct a thorough investigation extensively to find out exactly what happened and those involved. Other countries will also offer their assistance, this is a global priority, working around the clock. DARPA officials with military intelligence analyze the following, DNA from the dead bodies, blood samples from one of the sect believers, fingerprints from vehicles, tire dirt particles from the small cargo planes left abandoned, facial identifications from the airports, passport verifications, locations involved, weaponry involved. After all the data is processed, it is at this time without any doubt that these attacks were orchestrated by the daughter of the late Ron Ben Ruckman which was once a colleague and great scientific mind of DARPA. It is believed at this time that after the late DARPA scientist suffering from severe mental depression, after losing his pregnant wife in a blast that took many souls. He was radicalized by extreme radicals and became a messiah, he went on to mastermind a sophisticated attack on the DARPA compounds. At this time, some of the perpetrators were killed and some face the full force of the justice system. DARPA, had no choice but to eliminate the late Ron Ben Ruckman, so a sophisticated attack was returned in kindly. After the death of the late scientist and messiah, his daughter named Siria took over the role of leadership. Siria, was enraged with revenge and hatred towards DARPA, at this time Siria has become the most wanted international fugitive worldwide. We shall track Siria down and bring her to justice to face prosecution, we will track her down to the corners of the earth and work diligently 24 hours a day. A complete assessment of damages and those killed are as follows, many innocent lives were killed, tens of millions of dollars in damages, DARPA, lost countless of autonomous super soldiers. They is an outrage throughout the DARPA officials and the military, the mood is payback for those responsible.

CHAPTER 30

Soon afterwards, in every region especially the Middle East the raids began, these infamous raids were later called the DARPA raids. DARPA and military forces combined would raid entire cities, towns and villages, desperately looking for Siria and her believers. They would spare nobody to gather intel on any information, they use their most advanced technologies by air, land and sea. People were frightened by their presence, constantly watching the autonomous lethal supersonic drones hovering around. Watching the fleet of autonomous super soldiers, and by sea the autonomous weaponized aquatic drones. This was continuous and persistent, they were searching endlessly on a 24-hour basis. Before the raids began, DARPA was able to find the small cargo planes, take samples of the tires. They even tracked the tire marks from the vehicles, DARPA was extremely serious in apprehending anyone that assisted or our directly involved with the sect believers. The biggest prize would be Siria, but time kept ticking away, the frustration grew more and more. At this point, Isiah and the six sect believers were already healed and joined the others in extremely remote locations. The day Isiah and the six sect believers returned, they were in an underground cave system hiding with the group of sect believers and Siria. Isiah speaks, "my encounters with death have been many, death has always been my companion. The difference in battle is everyone wants to go home, I'm already home. The minute death respects you, there is a clear understanding forged. We believe in the ancient ideologies and will never be poisoned by the misrepresentation of modern ideologies." This pattern continued rotating from place to place in remote locations, one night Isiah was watching the stars above when suddenly Siria approaches him. Siria and Isiah embraced each other; it was as if destiny made a path for them. That night they soon became lovers, both of them have gone through so much pain in their lives. The other sect believers were always standing guard in their absence, everyone knew that Siria has fallen for Isiah. Something that was unthinkable actually happened, it seems that Siria admired his bravery and fearless perspectives. This continued for months, during that time DARPA and the military units kept the raids going vigorously. Going region to region, house to house, not leaving any rock unturned.

CHAPTER 31

One afternoon Isiah was getting some supplies in a nearby town away from the sect believer's groups and Siria. When suddenly, a DARPA raid is manifesting in the town where he is located. When suddenly, Isiah and some of the sect believers are being approached by the autonomous super soldiers. The moment Isiah was instantly recognized he threw some live grenades at the autonomous super soldiers. The blast did cause some damage but not enough to disable all their mechanisms. The other sect believers with Isiah also threw live grenades at the autonomous super soldiers. Same thing happened; the blast did cause some damage but not enough to disable them. The autonomous super soldiers returned fire instantly disintegrating Isiah and the other sect believers. The brave men were killed instantly, they died a good death, this moto rages among warriors throughout centuries. Isiah and some of the sect believers when on guard, always have an emergency small device with them in case of any emergency situations. Isiah, did manage to press the button to warn Siria and the other sect believers that something went terribly wrong. The minute they receive the signal, Siria knows that Isiah and the others are gone. With no hesitation, they quickly move within the hidden location out to another location. The groups of sect believers and Siria are moving using mostly herds of mules. The terrain in which they are located, it's rugged, but they do use vehicles (ep) electric powered which they keep close by to go and get supplies.

CHAPTER 32

By now, Siria knows she is pregnant and facing many challenges, a lot of the people that live in the area are mostly against modern technologies. This helps out a great deal when supplies are needed to any type of assistance. One night, Siria gathers with her most trusted loyalists, they gather around her sitting crisscross on the ground. Siria, tells her most trusted loyalists which already been told that she was pregnant. This conversation however, is about the divine name of her baby, they will be given two names in case of either gender. Abdul (servant of god) or Abdullah (servant of god), let it be known that these are the names that are chosen. The loyalists now have the honor to protect this child for futures to come, Siria, has chosen well, these names were given to her in a dream by the creator. No one knows what challenges the future will bring, but now there is hope for many generations to come. Ever since, the death of Isiah, Siria has been saddened, it seems that tragedy stays close to her, as a everlasting unwanted companion.

Chapter 33

After more time passes by, on a rainy, windy, even thunderstorms, early morning, as if nature was giving off signs. Siria, gives birth to a beautiful boy, that is full of life, unfortunately, that same day after a short time Siria dies from complications. Let's review a full list of speculations and theories will be examined at this time why Siria passed away after giving birth. Keep in mind, that to be 100% certain her body needs to be exhumed and examined properly, to find the complicated answers. Theory one, she was under so much stress and emotional pain that she had a severe hemorrhage, that couldn't be managed. Theory two, when she was a teenager and wanted to speak to her parents before passing away, she accidentally inhaled traces of tiny deadly chemical compositions, that later on manifested. Theory three, acute or chronic exposure to a toxic substance, known as the latency period. Theory four, a health condition (such as heart disease), or preeclampsia (a serious blood pressure condition that can happen after the 20th week of pregnancy or after giving birth). The world will never know, that same day she was buried in an unmarked grave inside the cave where she gave birth. Siria's most trusted loyalists and the groups of sect believers will protect this divine child and hide him from the world until he is much older. DARPA and the military personnel's will continue their endeavors, not knowing anything for futures to come. Only the future shall determine the paths moving forward, and the will of our creator for humanity.

www.ingramcontent.com/pod-product-compliance
Lightning Source LLC
Chambersburg PA
CBHW080923190726
48293CB00010B/2665